An
Elk
Dropped
In

An
Elk
Dropped
In

Andreas Steinhöfel

PICTURES BY Kerstin Meyer
TRANSLATED BY Alissa Jaffa

FRONT STREET
Asheville, North Carolina

First U.S. edition

Steinhöfel, Andreas.
[Es ist ein Elch entsprungen]
An elk dropped in / Andreas Steinhofel ; illustrated by Kerstin Meyer ; translated by Alisa Jaffa.
p. cm.
Summary: While on a pre-Christmas trial run for the famous man in red, an elk named
Mr. Moose crashes through the roof of a house and, while recuperating from a sprain, regales
Billy Wagner and his family with stories.
ISBN-13: 978-1-932425-80-2 (hardcover : alk. paper)
[1. Elk—Fiction. 2. Santa Claus—Fiction. 3. Christmas—Fiction.] I. Meyer, Kerstin, ill.
II. Jaffa, Alisa. III. Title.
PZ7.S82635Elk 2006
[Fic]—dc22
2006000804

Front Street
An Imprint of Boyds Mills Press, Inc.
A Highlights Company

815 Church Street
Honesdale, Pennsylvania 18431

An
Elk
Dropped
In

Mr. Moose Lands

It was just before Christmas when Mr. Moose landed on our house on Finches Way, the outermost road of our little German town. During Advent we sing carols to music in the living room. That's why we were there at the time: Kiki was sitting at the piano, Mama was playing the recorder, and I was responsible for the singing. (I have a boy-soprano voice.)

The room smelled of orange peel, which Mama had placed on the radiators. The warm glow of candles was mirrored in the windows, and outside soft snowflakes were silently drifting down to earth. I was in a very Christmassy mood.

"'Hark! The herald angels sing,'" I sang.

Mama removed the recorder from her lips and merrily warbled the chorus.

But it wasn't the angels that came down from heaven. It was Mr. Moose. There was a deafening crash, and the next moment there he was plunging through the ceiling. More precisely, *first* he plunged through the roof and *then* through the living-room ceiling. The floor shook under our feet. I heard Mama and Kiki scream.

In a hail of bricks and roof tiles a huge brown *thing* landed on Søren, reducing it to matchwood. Søren was our living-room table from IKEA. The Advent wreath and the coconut biscuits on it were crushed to bits.

The coconut biscuits didn't matter. Grandma had baked them and sent them by post. As usual, she'd let them burn. Every year Mama uses them for decorations until just before Christmas Eve, and then Kiki and I feed all of them to the ducks in the park. When Grandma comes to

stay over Christmas, we have to tell her how delicious they were. I don't like telling lies, but after all, the ducks do enjoy them.

"My God, what is it?" whispered Mama as the dust settled. The huge brown thing lay motionless in the middle of the debris, the splintered remains of Søren and the biscuit crumbs. It had antlers and four long legs pointing up to heaven in all directions.

"It's an elk," said Kiki. "A male, at that."

Showing off again. She had to prove her general knowledge could be relied upon even in times of crisis. It would probably earn her an extra Christmas present. An older sister can make life seem very unfair.

The elk's antlers were covered with soft velvet. They felt warm and cold at the same time.

"Billy Wagner, take your fingers off that creature!" ordered Mama. I jerked my hand away. Mama is afraid of fleas and lice. That's why I'm not allowed to have a dog, either.

"How d'you know it's a male?" she asked Kiki.

"Female elks don't have antlers," explained my sister.

"Oh yes," said Mama and nodded. "Of course."

Of course! Just as well Gertrude Wutherspoon didn't hear that. She's our neighbor and, since Mama's

divorce from Papa, her best friend. Every Thursday she attends the women's group and fights for emancipation.

Mama looked up at the enormous dark hole in the ceiling, with dust still floating down from its edges. "Do elks fly?" she asked in disbelief.

"No," said Kiki. "Nor do they go mountaineering, dive, or play tennis. And they can't talk, either."

As if he'd been waiting for just this moment, the elk opened his eyes. "That's where you're wrong, little girl!" he mumbled. "I speak five languages, and fluently, at that."

"Well, all right," replied Kiki, unfazed. "But you do have an American accent!"

She hates not having the last word.

Mama was standing ramrod straight, as if she'd just swallowed her recorder. Her mouth opened and then shut again. She simply wasn't used to having talking elks dropping onto her house.

"My name is Mr. Moose," the elk introduced himself. His voice was as soft as his antlers. "From the family of the Cervidae." He began to get up and became bigger and bigger. My head barely reached up to his neck, from which a shaggy tassel dangled like a beard.

"Cervidae are ruminants that shed their antlers annually," explained Kiki without anyone having asked her.

"Of course," said Mama again.

"Like reindeer, for example," added Kiki.

Mr. Moose cowered and drew his head in. "Are there any of those beasts here?" he snorted loudly.

"Of course *not!*" said Mama. "Now perhaps you'd be so kind as to explain just how you came to land here?"

I really admired her. She was even being polite to guests who had reduced her living room to a war zone and had Søren on their conscience.

"I swerved," replied Mr. Moose. "Got knocked off course over Ireland."

"You flew over by way of Ireland?"

"My actual destination was Scandinavia. The accident happened at the turnoff."

"It's quite a long way from Ireland."

"Centrifugal force," Kiki broke in. "He must have been going at quite a speed."

I found it really embarrassing the way she was flaunting her knowledge in front of Mr. Moose. Mama asked her to go and get her camera to photograph Mr. Moose and the spot where he landed so she could file for insurance.

"I feel terrible about having fallen on such an attractive woman's roof, madam," said Mr. Moose gallantly. "The Boss will of course pay for the damage caused."

The Boss?

It was a long time since anyone had given Mama a compliment. Perhaps that's why she ignored the last sentence.

"I suppose it's just a hole in the ceiling and one in the roof," she said. Her cheeks had flushed bright red with embarrassment. "Though it is getting a bit cold."

Hundreds of snowflakes were spinning down on us through these holes. In the photos Kiki took of us that evening it looks really pretty.

When the film was used up, Mama decided that

the holes had to be covered before we were completely
snowed over.

"I'll help you with the repairs," Mr. Moose offered
generously. "But I'm afraid I've sprained my left front
leg."

Now that was right up Mama's alley! She loves it
when someone is ill or hurts themselves. If she had
her way, I'd come down with chicken pox or mumps
three times a year.

"You're going to stay in the garage until you're
better," Mama ordered Mr. Moose. The garage has
been empty since Papa got the car after the divorce.
"And later on I'll make you some cold compresses."

I was jealous of Kiki, who was allowed to bring the limping Mr. Moose outside, while I had to climb up to the boring old attic with Mama. We placed boards across the hole in the living-room ceiling and then nailed a thick plastic sheet under the hole in the roof.

"Can Mr. Moose stay with us?" I asked.

"Well, at least until his ankle is better," said Mama. "After that we'll see."

Papa once said you should never wish for anything bad to happen. But as I was hammering a nail into the plastic, I secretly wished that Mr. Moose's ankle would take a very long time to heal.

That evening we all went to bed late. Although I was very tired, I couldn't get to sleep. I could hear the plastic awning in the attic flapping softly in the winter wind. Once I was sure that Mama and Kiki were asleep, I took my torch, put on my coat and boots, and plodded through the snow-covered garden to the garage.

Mr. Moose was still awake as well. He blinked in the light from my torch. There were three kitchen towels wrapped round his left front leg.

"I have a question, Mr. Moose," I said.

"I'll answer you once you've given me a scratch behind my right ear, little boy," he said.

His ears were bigger than my hands; the fur behind them was warm and soft. It smelled a bit like the zoo or a horse's stable.

Mr. Moose grunted contentedly. "Where's your daddy?" he asked after a while.

"I don't know. Gertrude Wutherspoon says he's gone to the devil."

"Aha, down south. D'you miss him?"

Whenever I thought of Papa, I got a funny sort of cramp in my stomach and felt dizzy. I didn't like to talk about it.

"Mr. Moose," I said, "who is *the Boss?*"

"The Boss," mumbled Mr. Moose. He limped past me to the garage door and stared out into the dark winter sky. "Didn't I say? The Boss is Santa Claus, of course."

"Santer who?" I asked.

"Santa Claus," repeated Mr. Moose. He turned round to me, so that I could look straight into his beautiful brown eyes. "At any rate that's his American name. You call him Father Christmas."

Mr. Moose Is Discovered

I remember Father Christmas very well. Last year he suddenly appeared on our doorstep promptly on the twenty-fourth of December. He didn't say a word as he stepped out of the cold and dark into the hall. His red coat was dotted with small snowflakes. They melted like they were on a hot plate.

I was feeling a bit scared. I'd been rather naughty. That summer I'd picked up firecrackers left over from New Year's Eve and set them off in Pannecke's hen coop and broken twenty-three eggs. I guessed that Father Christmas had known every single egg in person.

"Are you frightened, Billy Wagner?" he asked.

"Yes," I said.

"So you should be!" he roared and rushed Mama, Kiki, and me through the apartment, swinging his broomstick made of tied-up twigs. I screeched in terror.

We fled to the living room, where we twirled three times round the beautifully decorated Christmas tree. Then Mama dropped onto the sofa. Father Christmas fell on top of her and plastered her with kisses.

"Gary," laughed Mama, "not in front of the children!"

Kiki was laughing as well. She'd known all the time.

I may have been little, but I wasn't stupid. I knew that Father Christmas wasn't called Gary, and that apart from Papa no other man in the world was allowed to kiss Mama. That's how I discovered that Father Christmas doesn't exist. I was very disappointed.

I was even more disappointed when not long after that Mama and Papa got divorced and Papa moved out. Apparently all that kissing hadn't done any good. It wasn't much of a consolation, but at least the

business with the smashed chickens' eggs didn't get found out.

"Father Christmas doesn't exist," I said defiantly to Mr. Moose that night in the garage. "Nor does Santerclaws."

"Yes, he does," said Mr. Moose softly. "And now stop crying. It breaks my heart to see little boys cry."

Next morning after breakfast I pestered Kiki to come to the garage, and asked Mr. Moose to tell her about the Boss. I was sure that Kiki wouldn't believe in Santerclaws. I was mistaken.

"Scientists have to believe in everything, until the opposite has been proved," she said. "Just because Father Christmas has never appeared on a talk show doesn't mean he doesn't exist."

"Quite right, little girl," mumbled Mr. Moose.

Like it or not, I had to admit that Kiki was making a big impression on him. A jealous yellow bird fluttered in my heart. I wanted Mr. Moose all to myself as a friend.

Mama appeared with fresh cold compresses. She asked Mr. Moose if he was hungry and what he would like to eat.

"A little mozzarella with tomatoes as a starter,

followed by spinach pizza with no garlic. And a light Italian white wine to go with it," Mr. Moose said. Mama's eyes became as big as saucers.

"But if you don't have all that, dry hay will do." Mr. Moose gave a grin, showing his enormous white teeth. "And some fruit for dessert … poached pears would do very nicely."

"We should be able to get hold of some hay," muttered Mama in relief. "I could try the riding stables. No, better phone Pannecke. He's got a farm."

Two hours later a muted rumbling could be heard in the street. Wrapped in a padded coat, old Pannecke clattered into our drive on his tractor. His bald head was covered with a fur cap far too big for him that kept slipping down onto his forehead.

"Pannecke always delivers on time," he called good-naturedly.

I climbed up onto the trailer, where eight huge bales of hay covered the floor, and helped him unload. Pannecke grinned at me. Immediately I had a guilty conscience. Ever since Mr. Moose landed, one thing or another kept reminding me of the twenty-three broken eggs.

"I'll carry the bales into the garage for you," said

Pannecke once we'd finished unloading. "All part of the service."

"The garage is a mess," called Mama. Her face went bright red. And she stuttered, saying *"gagagarage."*

Old Pannecke pushed his fur hat to the back of his head, stuck his nose up in the air, and sniffed. I suddenly remembered that he was a keen big game hunter. Mr. Moose certainly wouldn't want to end up a fur cap on Pannecke's bald head.

"What have you got in there, then? What's in the garage?" asked Pannecke suspiciously. "Something

smells a bit strong. And what d'you need the hay for?"

Mama looked at Kiki and me for help. She's no good at lying. She leaves that to us, like with Grandma's coconut biscuits.

"We're building scenery for the stable in Bethlehem," said Kiki, "for a Nativity play. We may come back to you, if we need a few animals. Cows, sheep, and that."

"Pigs," said Mama eagerly.

Kiki gave a quiet sigh. Even I knew that the stable

in Bethlehem didn't have pigs in it. Otherwise they'd be on the Advent calendars.

"Yeah, well, I might have a sheep to spare," muttered Pannecke in a baffled tone of voice. He looked one last time in the direction of the garage, then tipped the brim of his fur cap, climbed up on the tractor and puttered off.

Mama, Kiki, and I gave a sigh of relief. We had decided not to breathe a single word to anyone about Mr. Moose. Mama said that in any case no one would believe her if she told them about a flying elk. Kiki wanted to collect all known scientific facts about talking ruminants and Santerclaws before going public. And I still wanted Mr. Moose all to myself.

But naturally everything turned out differently.

It started with Gertrude Wutherspoon going to look for an oilcan in the garage. Because she's Mama's best friend, she has her own key. Suddenly, just before lunch, there she was in our kitchen. She was wrapped in at least twenty silk scarves, all hand-painted by herself.

"Kirsten Wagner," she said to Mama, who was just cooking spaghetti for us, "there's an elk standing in your garage."

"Well, I never," said Mama quite casually, dropping the wooden cooking spoon into the spaghetti sauce. "How on earth did it get there?"

"How it got there, I've no idea," said Gertrude. "But he's asking what happened to his poached pears."

There was no choice, we had to explain. We told her everything, except that neither Kiki nor I mentioned the Boss.

"You are quite impossible, Kirsten," said Gertrude as we were making for the garage. Mama was carrying a bowl of poached pears. "You've hardly been divorced a year, and here you are serving a man with food again!"

That wasn't true, as *I* was the one who'd been carrying most of the food for Mr. Moose into the garage. He'd already gobbled up half the first bale of hay.

"I'm pleased to meet you," he said as Mama introduced Gertrude Wutherspoon to him. "What charming scarves you're wearing!"

"Your soft-soaping doesn't wash with me," said Gertrude.

I explained to Mr. Moose that Gertrude Wutherspoon was fighting for emancipation. Mr. Moose wanted to

know what that meant. Gertrude explained that an example of emancipation would be if a female elk also wanted antlers.

"My dear, that is a perfectly absurd idea," said Mr. Moose.

"My dear," retorted Gertrude, "you are a victim of the filthy male-oriented system." Then she picked up the oilcan that she needed for her environmentally friendly flour mill and went back into the house with Mama.

Gertrude Wutherspoon didn't particularly take to Mr. Moose, at least not at first. She told Mama he was a tough guy. All the same, she never told a soul about him. I'll always be grateful to her for that, and that's why I'm also in favor of emancipation now.

That afternoon Kiki decided the time had come to do some serious scientific research on Mr. Moose and ask him some questions. She took a notebook and freshly sharpened pencil with her to the garage.

"Mr. Moose," she began, "what is the nature of your connection with Santa Claus, and does this relationship have anything to do with your falling onto our house at Number Four Finches Way?"

I must say the question sounded very scientific, but I'd have been far more interested to know whether Mr. Moose liked jelly bears.

"That's a long story," said Mr. Moose. "How much time do you have?"

We made ourselves comfortable. I snuggled up against Mr. Moose's warm fur and tickled him behind his huge ears. With pencil poised, Kiki sat on a heap of old car tires as Mr. Moose began.

He hadn't exaggerated. It really was a long story.

Mr. Moose Tells His Story

The world is a big place and Christmas comes but once a year, which meant Santa Claus was really hard pressed doing everything necessary and getting it done all in one day. So at some point he decided to distribute presents on Christmas Eve in some countries—as he does over here in Germany—and not till the next day, like in America and Great Britain.

I interrupted Mr. Moose. Up to now I'd always thought Baby Jesus arrived on Christmas Eve the world over. Mr. Moose shook his head. He said that the Baby Jesus was well known to Santerclaws and had his head full of nonsense. For example, sometimes the Little Child decided to give men and boys broken suspenders and fell about laughing when their trousers fell down in the street.

There are just too many children in America for Santa Claus to visit every single house on foot. Well, he could if he wanted to, but what's his sled for? That contraption is an absolute miracle! Even the tiniest parts are carved from delicately worked wood, and the little bells and the runners are made of pure silver. Despite the staggering load it carries, in favorable weather conditions the sled goes as fast as ... well, it's very fast. And why? Because it's pulled—pulled along by a number of reindeer, who were given this responsible job long, long ago.

At this point, Mr. Moose bared his teeth, before counting out eight names. I can remember only four of them: Dasher, Comet, Donner, and Blitzen. Kiki wrote down the rest, but Mr. Moose said it wasn't necessary. In America apparently every child knows them all.

You'd think the reindeer would be pleased and grateful to be allowed to help the Boss. But I have to tell you— gratitude, not a bit of it! Those creatures are arrogant and conceited. They won't have anything to do with someone like me! Only eat the finest food, when they aren't busy

*grooming their fur and having their antlers polished to a
shine. They even have their hooves polished, and if everything isn't exactly right, then they refuse to pull the sled!
You know, there'd be millions of innocent children crying
their eyes out if there weren't any presents on Christmas,
and they're quite shameless the way they take advantage
of it.*

Later on Kiki showed me a picture of a reindeer.
It was far more dainty than Mr. Moose, had lighter-
colored fur and very beautiful eyes. It couldn't have
been one of Santerclaws's reindeers, as its antlers were
rather grubby.

*As far as the sled's concerned—and this is where we
get to the nub of it all—obviously it only gets used once*

a year, at Christmastime. The rest of the time it's left standing around practically useless, and then one of the bolts may come loose, a little bell may jam, the runners need to be re-covered, and the reins inspected. All in all it's a load of work, so in the run-up to Christmas a complete overhaul takes place. Then there's a trial run—and this is where we elks come into the picture.

Kiki was busily scribbling all this down.

Since my lords the reindeer consider themselves far too grand to make the trial runs (they're always just males, by the way—so much for your emancipation thingam-ajig), the Boss always falls back on me and three buddies. I have to admit, we elks aren't the best of runners. But we do have stamina and strength. A major cold-weather

front doesn't immediately make us go belly-up. Nor should it, for trial drives are not without danger—otherwise, I'd never have gone off course over Ireland if one of the silver runners hadn't shot across a rain cloud! And yet we're happy to do it. After all, what other elk gets to see as

much of the world as we do—and from the air at that!
Yes, it's a great honor working for Santa Claus, a great
honor ...

Mr. Moose sounded a bit sad as he told us this. It
upset him that the whole world knew about reindeer

and adored them, but no one ever mentioned the elks.

My dream is that one day I'll be allowed to go on the great Christmas run—when the sled is working properly and glides along as if on feathers so that you hardly feel its weight and the cold snow flies past your ears. But, of course, there's no chance of that, as none of the reindeer would ever permit it. Nor would the Boss. He's a great one for tradition. He's a nice enough old fellow, but if you contradict him he can turn quite nasty. I wonder whether he's missing me.

Of course, the most important question of all was how this business with the flying worked. Unfortunately, the little information Mr. Moose could give us was rather disappointing.

Professional secret—not mine, but the Boss's! How he manages to do it, lifting what amounts to three hundred kilos live weight per reindeer plus the sled loaded with all those presents up into the air, I don't rightly know. I have a vague idea it has something to do with the dust from the Milky Way that he carries around with him in little cloth bags. ... Whatever, without the Boss's help, I can't fly. Talking is another matter. Once you've learned it, you never forget. But flying without the Milky Way Powder simply isn't possible. Otherwise, I'd have invited you for a little air tour long ago.

Kiki snapped her notebook shut. She still had a load of questions for Mr. Moose, but she wanted to leave them for another time. Together we watched Mr. Moose as he polished off the next load of hay and two poached pears. Later on I discovered that he did like jelly bears, preferably green and red ones.

That evening I fell asleep right away. I dreamed about Santerclaws and his sled. We were shooting through the black night sky and through whirling snowflakes, pulled along by Mr. Moose and his friends. Mr. Moose was laughing happily, and whenever his strong hooves touched the clouds, they sprayed golden sparks into the winter sky.

Mr. Moose Rides Out

During the next few days, Finches Way was filled with the loud noise of banging and hammering. Mama had called in the builders to repair the roof and the living-room ceiling. Kiki took care of the men, who were all very curious and wanted to know how the damage had happened.

"A meteorite," she called out eagerly. "It came out of the cosmos. It was gigantic."

Wrapped in a heavy winter coat, she sat on the roof and told the workmen everything she knew about meteorites and the cosmos. It took hours. After that, the men stopped asking her questions.

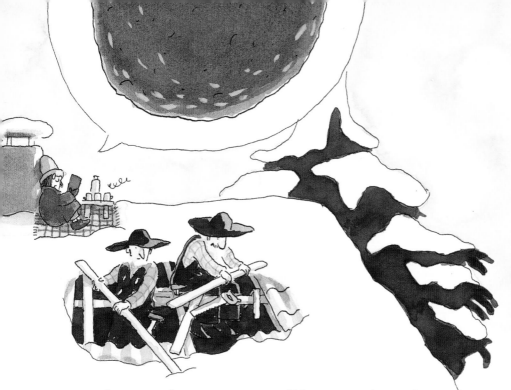

Kiki wanted Mr. Moose to tell her everything about the lives of elks. She filled one notebook after another with her scribbling and used up several pencils.

In the afternoons she then typed everything out neatly on the typewriter.

"Little one, you're very clever," Mr. Moose said to her once.

Kiki replied that she'd love to go to Paris with him and introduce him to the members of the Académie française, because they were the cleverest men in the world.

"Ah, Paris," said Mr. Moose enthusiastically.

"Once we very nearly crashed the sled into the Eiffel Tower."

"An accident!" I shouted.

"Almost," said Mr. Moose. "The last real accident the Boss had happened several hundred years ago. That was in a small Italian town called Pisa."

The days with Mr. Moose passed all too quickly. Because he often felt lonely, I spent most of the time together with him in the garage. There I listened to his stories. He told me about the sparkling waters of the river Nile and the green canopies of the rain forests. He'd seen the snow-covered peak of Mount Everest and the thundering Niagara waterfall. He knew the sun-scorched deserts of Africa and the eternal ice of the northern seas. "The world is a precious miracle," said Mr. Moose.

He was in great form, for under Mama's attentive care his leg was healing quickly, and he was thrilled with her poached pears.

"You're slurping, Mr. Moose," Mama rebuked him on one occasion. "It sounds like when you give a baby a smack on its bare bottom."

"You shouldn't smack children," replied Mr. Moose.

Later on he admitted to me that he'd been terribly embarrassed by the slurping business.

Now and again Gertrude Wutherspoon came by. She was determined to get Mr. Moose interested in the emancipation of female elks. Mr. Moose discussed it with her but wouldn't let himself be won over. But he never forgot to compliment Gertrude on her colorful silk scarves.

"He really is the nicest fellow I know," said Gertrude Wutherspoon to Mama.

Once I saw her slipping Mr. Moose home-baked whole meal bread rolls with cottage cheese. She begged him not to let anyone know about it, otherwise she'd get thrown out of the women's group.

"Word of honor, my dear," Mr. Moose assured her, and indeed he never mentioned the whole meal roll and cottage cheese to me. He was very gallant.

One evening Mama invited Mr. Moose for a special dinner. He was a bit nervous as he came limping out of the garage into the house. During the meal he didn't slurp once, but while he was eating the fruit salad, he unintentionally let slip a loud burp.

"Madam, I am most dreadfully sorry," said Mr. Moose.

"Burping isn't quite so bad," said Mama.

After dinner we all watched a feature film on television that deeply impressed Mr. Moose. The film was called *Casablanca*. It's about a man and a woman who don't end up together although they love each other. Because they're both very unhappy, they play the piano all the time. In the end the woman flies off in an airplane and the man stays behind in Casablanca.

"I'm very moved," said Mr. Moose when the film was over.

Mama was moved as well. She screwed up a tissue she'd been weeping into. Even Kiki was sniffing a bit. The man and the woman had said that maybe they would meet again one day in Paris. Kiki found that terribly romantic.

It was a wonderful evening. The living room glowed with the light from loads of candles and Mr. Moose sang us some American Christmas carols. His deep bass voice made some of the glasses in the wall cupboard tinkle. Then Kiki and I were allowed to hang the Christmas tree baubles and decorations on his antlers. Mama took a photo. The photo shows Kiki on the left, me on the right, and between us Mr. Moose smiling good-naturedly.

I'll never forget the day Mr. Moose announced his leg was now completely better. He went out into the garden, where his heavy hooves left deep prints in the snow. His soft muzzle sniffed at every tree and every bush.

"Smells quite different than it does back in America," he said.

He had told me about America. Where Mr. Moose came from there were endless broad, green valleys, and clear rivers rushing out of deep crevices in the mountains.

"Are you homesick, Mr. Moose?" I asked.

He shook his head with its huge antlers. "Working for the Boss has turned me into a globe-trotter. Wherever I rest my antlers, that's my home."

I really liked the sound of that. Mr. Moose explained it was a motto of the North American elks.

He rummaged in the snow a bit more, nibbling at the bark of an apple tree and enjoying the warmth of the winter sun. Then suddenly he came to a halt in front of the low hedge that separates our garden from the wood behind it and stood there thoughtfully.

"Little boy," he said, "would you like to come for a ride through the woods with me?"

"Yes!" I replied, my heart pounding with excitement.

"Then climb up on my back and hold on tight," said Mr. Moose as he sank awkwardly to his knees. "And don't be afraid, I'll take care of you."

I swung myself across his back, bent forward, and wrapped my arms around his big, warm neck.

"Let's go!" I whispered in his right ear.

Mr. Moose carefully lifted his long legs over the hedge. He began to trot. Then he ran, and as he picked up speed we stormed through the snow-covered winter woods, with the trees whooshing past us like shadows.

"Faster, Mr. Moose!" I yelled. "Faster, faster, carry me away!"

The white of the snow danced with the blue of the sky. I laughed and laughed, the cold wind tousled my hair, and Mr. Moose simply flew along.

Not once did he stumble over even the sharpest rise in the woodland floor, at no point was I touched or scratched by the snow-laden branches hanging down from the trees. And I was never afraid, because Mr. Moose was taking care of me.

"Fantastic to be able to run like this again at last!"

he said as he stopped at a clearing in the middle of the woods. "Apart from wanting to pull the Christmas sled, this has been my deepest wish. Little boy, what's *your* deepest wish?"

I realized he didn't mean the kind of present like a fully automatic electric juicer that Kiki and I were going to give Mama for Christmas. My heart was beating because I had never before told anyone what my deepest wish was. It was an even bigger secret than breaking Pannecke's eggs.

"I wish," I said, "that we were a family again with a papa."

Mr. Moose considered that an excellent wish. He wanted to know why Mama and Papa were divorced. I couldn't really explain properly. Mama once said that she and Papa had loved each other, but hadn't understood each other. She'd said that sometimes people had to go their separate ways.

"That's sad but true," said Mr. Moose.

I found it very sad as well. It was rather like in

that *Casablanca* film, except that Mama and Papa hadn't played the piano all the time before they were divorced.

"I'll tell the Boss about your wish," said Mr. Moose. "I promise you!"

All of a sudden I felt very dejected. Mr. Moose had said out loud what I'd been thinking about for quite a while: as his leg was now healed he would leave us and go back to Santerclaws in America. I didn't dare ask when that would be, because I was so afraid of the answer.

And so Mr. Moose and I returned in silence to Finches Way on this wonderful, sunny winter's day.

A Visitor for Mr. Moose

Two days before Christmas Eve, Grandma arrived for
her annual Christmas visit, loaded with bags and suit-
cases. We had intended to prepare her very slowly for
Mr. Moose.

"I don't have to tell you why," Mama had said.

"The hat," Kiki had replied.

Long ago Grandma had been attacked by a giraffe
that had eaten her expensive straw hat with plastic
apples on it right off her head. Ever since, she's been
terrified of large animals. To prevent her coming across
Mr. Moose by chance on her very first day, Mama had
asked him if he minded being kept carefully locked up

in the garage. He didn't.

"Oh, a new table," Grandma noticed when we all settled down in the living room for afternoon tea. "How pretty. And very sturdy."

The name of the new table was Flipskøken. It was made of tough beechwood. Mama said only an elephant crashing down on it would make it fall to bits.

Grandma straightened the little hat she wore for traveling. This one wasn't made of straw, but some flimsy green material and looked like a battered bird's nest. "Are there any of my coconut biscuits left?" she asked.

"We finished those up ages ago," said Kiki with a beaming smile. "They were absolutely delicious."

I nodded and beamed as well and was thinking of the poor ducks in the park who had had to do without this year.

"I could manage a little drink," said Grandma, pulling her hat about on her head. "I find train journeys so exhausting."

Kiki grinned. We all knew that Grandma liked a little drink even when she *hadn't* just been on a train journey. That's why Mama had bought two bottles of cherry brandy on her last shopping trip, one of which she now placed on Flipskøken.

"Ah, a sip of cherry brandy!" said Grandma, and rubbed her hands together in delight.

At this moment the doorbell rang.

"Kiki, Billy, would you answer the door?" said Mama.

When we opened it there was an old man in an old-fashioned check suit standing on the doorstep. He had white hair, bright blue eyes, and a big belly. He looked very friendly, but he wasn't.

"I've come to fetch my elk," he said. "My name is Santa Claus."

"Can you prove it?" I asked coldly.

"Of course I can prove it," said the old man. "You are Billy Wagner, and the summer before last you broke twenty-three eggs in Pannecke's hen coop."

"Billy!" gasped Kiki in admiration.

I felt so awful, I wanted to sit down. Not a soul in the whole wide world knew about the business with the hens' eggs. I hadn't even told Mr. Moose about it.

The old man was *the Boss!*

"I am fully aware that the elk is tucked away in your garage," said Santerclaws. "But it's locked. So may I ask you to be so good as to let me have the key?"

"You may not," came a voice from behind me. Mama

had stepped out into the hall with Grandma. "Who are you, anyway?"

"I'm Father Christmas!" growled Santerclaws.

"Oh," said Mama. "Can you prove it?"

"Of course I can prove it," said Santerclaws. "You are Kirsten Wagner, and every year you let your children feed their grandmother's coconut biscuits to the ducks in the park."

Mama turned very pale.

"Is that true?" shouted Grandma indignantly.

"Yes," said Santerclaws. "But you can't really blame her. The biscuits are always burnt."

Kiki opened her mouth to say something but thought better of it. That still makes me angry when I think about it. Who knows what secrets of hers Santerclaws might have revealed.

"Where's your sled?" I asked. I was playing for time, but I was curious as well.

Santerclaws explained that the sled was at home back in America, where it was being fitted out for the big Christmas ride. He had just come in a perfectly normal airplane and wanted Mr. Moose to fly back with him.

"In an airplane?" I asked.

"Well, of course not—he'll fly on his own," said Santerclaws. "And there's not a moment to lose. So come on, right away now, and bring out the elk, or else there'll be no Christmas presents!"

"What elk?" asked Grandma nervously.

"I'll explain later," replied Mama.

All the Christmas presents in the world didn't matter a scrap to me. I had nothing to lose apart from Mr. Moose, my best and only friend. "You can keep your Christmas presents!" I shouted. "I wouldn't take them from a kidnapper anyway!"

"That's for starters," said Mama, "and secondly, I buy all the Christmas presents myself."

"Buy, buy, buy," snapped Santerclaws. "All you humans think about is money and shopping! I'm not talking about presents you can *buy*. I'm talking about people's deepest felt wishes, which can only come true for those who believe in me."

"The elk stays here," said Mama firmly.

I was wondering whether Mr. Moose shouldn't be the one to decide for himself whether he wanted to go with his boss or not. It could be that would spare us a lot of bother as Santerclaws's ears were beginning to turn bright red. His blue eyes looked as if a storm was brewing in them that would break out at any moment.

"Do you want me to lose my temper?" he growled.

It suddenly occurred to me that he might be able to cast a spell over us. Mr. Moose hadn't mentioned anything like that, but then I'd never asked him. So there was still the possibility that Santerclaws might turn us all into burnt coconut biscuits—which, for a change, might not be fed to the ducks in the park but to Pannecke's hens in revenge. The idea was terrifying.

It was Grandma who saved the situation. "My good man," she said, smiling at Santerclaws, "before you get upset, why don't we have a little glass of cherry brandy? That works wonders."

"If you wish, madam," said Santerclaws. "But just a very little one."

When he chose to, he could be every bit as polite as Mr. Moose.

Half an hour later Grandma and Santerclaws were sitting in front of Flipskøken facing an empty bottle of cherry brandy. They were singing a song together about why it was so lovely down by the riverside. Before that, Santerclaws had explained to Grandma

that she needed to bake her coconut biscuits at a lower heat, and that she ought to buy herself a prettier hat.

"Honesty is the best policy," said Mama. "Kiki, bring in the second bottle of cherry brandy."

I asked Mama for the key to the garage and went out to Mr. Moose. He wasn't at all surprised that the Boss had come to fetch him.

"I ought to go with him," he said. "On the other hand, it would be nice to stay with you a little longer. I'll have to think about it."

It was already dark by the time Santerclaws finally

left. He was singing merrily as he swayed down Finches Way by the light of the street lamps in the direction of the town. He seemed to have forgotten all about Mr. Moose.

"He'll come back tomorrow," said Mr. Moose. "I can think it over till then."

Mr. Moose Flies Off

Next morning we heard the awful news on the radio. It was announced that an old man in a check suit singing at the top of his voice had been picked up by the police. The old man was obviously mentally disturbed as he maintained he was Father Christmas. For this reason he had been admitted to a psychiatric institution.

"What's a *psychiatric institution?*" I asked.

"A lunatic asylum," said Mama.

"The loony bin," said Grandma.

"It's a mental clinic," Kiki explained to Mr. Moose, who was listening attentively in the garage. "And once you're in there, you don't get out again that easily."

"So what?" I said. "What's so bad about that?" I wasn't that taken with Santerclaws. He hadn't behaved very well toward us. He'd come to take Mr. Moose. He'd given away all our secrets. He might even have turned us all into burnt biscuits. It seemed only right to me that he was tucked away in the loony bin now.

"But little boy," shouted Mr. Moose, "tomorrow night is Christmas Eve. If the Boss stays locked away, there'll be no Christmas!"

I understood right away what he meant by that. If there was no Christmas, everybody's heartfelt desires wouldn't be fulfilled anywhere in the world. "That's really terrible," I whispered.

A fully automatic electric juicer, like the one hidden under my bed, wasn't a heartfelt desire. A heartfelt desire is for peace on earth, that the man and the woman from *Casablanca* end up together, making everyone happy.

"If only I were allowed to fly," said Mr. Moose. "I'd crash through the roof of that clinic, snatch the Boss, and beat it!"

He shook his head worriedly, and the tassel under his chin swung sadly from side to side. The situation seemed hopeless. We were really desperate.

Mama hit on the idea of driving over to the clinic. As she didn't have a car of her own, Gertrude Wutherspoon drove her all the way to the other end of town in her little black Mini. An hour later they were back without having achieved anything.

"They wanted to lock me away!" shouted Mama furiously.

"Well, you really shouldn't have ordered the doctor to let Father Christmas go immediately," said Gertrude. "That really was stupid of you, Kirsten Wagner!"

When Kiki and I told Mr. Moose what had happened, he began to cry. Enormous tears rolled down from his beautiful eyes to his dark fur.

"It's all my fault," he said unhappily. "I should never have crash-landed. I'm a disgrace to the family of the Cervidae."

He backed into the farthest corner of the garage, where he curled himself up into a dark ball. I offered him green and red jelly bears and tickled him behind his drooping ears. But nothing and no one could comfort Mr. Moose. By the afternoon we still didn't know how we could set Santerclaws free. Mama was in the kitchen, cooking a bowl of poached pears in order to cheer Mr. Moose up. Kiki and I were in the sitting room with

Grandma, who needed a little drink of cherry brandy because of all the excitement.

"Poor Father Christmas," she sighed. "And I meant to give this back to him. It must have fallen out of his pocket."

She held something out for us to see. It was a tiny brown cloth bag. *Milky Way Powder!* "I'll keep it to remind me of him," said Grandma.

"That doesn't belong to Father Christmas, it's mine," said Kiki. She can tell a lie without batting an eyelid. Mama maintains she'll go far in this world.

"If it belongs to you," said Grandma, glaring, "then you must know what's inside it."

"Of course I do," replied Kiki sweetly. "It's got dried giraffe poo from the zoo in it."

Grandma screamed and dropped the little cloth bag in horror. Ten seconds later Kiki and I were in the garage with Mr. Moose.

"Yes, it really is Milky Way Powder," he said after he'd peeped into the little bag. "Now I can fly to the clinic and set the Boss free!"

"You'll have to take us with you, Mr. Moose," I said. "You won't find your way without us."

"Right you are," said Mr. Moose. "But quick, we

haven't a moment to lose! Sprinkle the Milky Way Powder over me, little boy."

"How?"

"Just imagine the little bag is a pepper pot and Mr. Moose a steak," said Kiki.

"Well, I don't think so!" grunted Mr. Moose, offended.

I shook the Milky Way Powder over his fur. The pale little grains did actually look like pepper. It was only when you looked at them closely that you could see they sparkled a little bit.

Mr. Moose went down on his knees so that Kiki and I could climb up on his back. "Off we go," he said.

But we didn't, because standing outside on the

snow-covered drive was old Pannecke. His fur cap had slipped far down onto his forehead, making him look very funny. But what didn't look funny at all was the shotgun he was holding in his hands.

"Nativity play indeed!" he shouted. "You've been hiding that elk! I spotted his footprints in the wood!"

"Mr. Pannecke, sir, please let us pass," I called. "Otherwise there's not going to be any Christmas!"

Old Pannecke just laughed. He positioned the shotgun and aimed at Mr. Moose. I was terrified. But just like Kiki, sitting behind me, I didn't move. If we remained sitting on Mr. Moose, Pannecke might not shoot.

"Get down," he growled. "I want some elk antlers and these will do nicely."

"The best you'll get is a pair on your silly hat," muttered Mr. Moose.

Pannecke had never heard an elk speak before. His eyes opened wide and he lowered the gun. Then he stood motionless, as if he'd turned to stone.

"Gack," he said.

"Gack?" repeated Mr. Moose. "What's a *gack*?"

"He thinks he's one of his own chickens," said Kiki.

Later she explained to me that old Pannecke had gone into shock. That was why he didn't move, even as Mr. Moose scraped his hooves sharply on the ground several times and then shot past him down the drive.

"Hold on tight," mumbled Mr. Moose, and a moment later he rose up from the ground and the wind was rushing past our ears. I had a feeling in my stomach like I got when Papa used to play airplanes with me and whirled me around in the air.

"We're flying!" I yelled.

"Don't look down," called Mr. Moose, "or else you'll get dizzy."

But I did look down. Our shadows slid over Mama, who was coming out of the house with a bowl of poached pears. She looked up and saw us flying off. Then Mr. Moose changed direction and Mama disappeared.

There is nothing to compare with flying on Mr. Moose's back. It was like our ride through the winter woods, but this time we were *flying*. The cold wind brought tears to my eyes, but I couldn't stop looking around.

The town below us looked tiny, really tiny. The houses and the cars were like the pieces of a toy village.

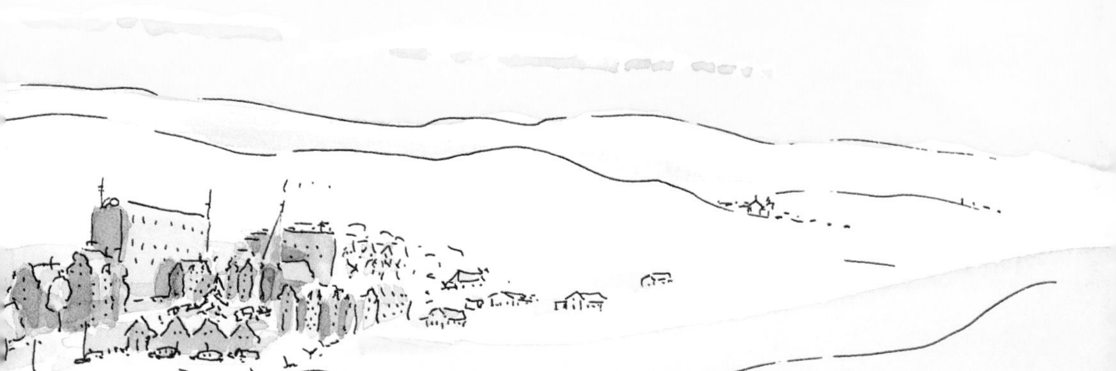

I recognized the school and the railway station. I saw the ice rink, with the people gliding across it like tiny colored dots.

"Look!" yelled Kiki.

She was pointing ahead. In the far distance, behind snow-covered, rolling hills, the sun was sinking like a flaming ball. Its light sent magical red outlines around the fluffy clouds. The whole world, the hills and the trees, the rivers and lakes, everything was suddenly covered with a rosy shimmer.

"Oh, Mr. Moose!" I called and felt so happy.

"Yes," he murmured. "I know, little boy."

We hadn't been flying long when it began to snow and my ears were feeling very cold. I was glad that soon after that we spotted the clinic. It stood on a hill at the edge of the forest. Its little battlements, tall gabled roof, and four chimneys made it look like a castle.

"You'll have to put us down somewhere before you crash through the roof, Mr. Moose!" called Kiki.

But we didn't have to get down and Mr. Moose didn't have to drop through the roof. That wasn't necessary because Santerclaws was sitting *on* the roof between two chimneys. Down in the courtyard of the clinic men and women doctors in white coats were running

about and pointing up at him in great agitation.

"Hello!" called Santerclaws, waving at us. Mr. Moose turned an elegant curve as he swooped down toward the roof. Right next to Santerclaws he stopped in midair, just as if he had firm ground under his hooves.

"Kindly get on, Boss," he puffed as some snowflakes danced in front of his nostrils.

"My faithful Moose!" yelled Santerclaws. His check suit and rosy old face were covered in soot. He clambered up awkwardly onto Mr. Moose's back and sat down behind Kiki and me. It was a bit of a squash, because he was so fat. I noticed that Santerclaws smelled like a chimney sweep.

"I skedaddled up the chimney in the doctor's office," he explained. "After all, climbing chimneys is my specialty."

"Well done, Boss," mumbled Mr. Moose. He did an almost vertical takeoff over the rooftop, snorted briefly, and sped away.

"Ho! Ho! Ho!" shouted Santerclaws in delight, and then we swept through the sky and the snowdrifts on the back of faithful Mr. Moose, who as far as I'm concerned is the greatest hero in the world.

Mr. Moose Flies Away

It was already getting dark and the town was twinkling like a mysterious carpet of lights as Mr. Moose landed us on Finches Way. He touched down gently in the garden and immediately Mama and Gertrude Wutherspoon came storming toward us.

"You could have crashed!" shouted Mama.

"Not with Mr. Moose," replied Mr. Moose confidently.

"He's a star!" said Gertrude.

Old Pannecke and his shotgun had gone. Mama had convinced him he'd had a bad dream and sent him back to his chickens. It had been snowing again so heavily that no one could spot Mr. Moose's tracks in the woods.

"I've been terribly worried about you," said Mama. "Enough to make me phone Papa. He'll be here tomorrow."

"Your mother's really lost it," said Gertrude. She was so upset that she'd tangled all her silk scarves up in knots.

I'd have loved to have had something to tie in knots myself. Papa was coming! I was tingling from my toes to my fingertips. Even Kiki was grinning all over her face. That was most unusual. As a rule she only ever does that when she's just gotten away with telling a lie.

"Don't build your hopes up too much," said Mama softly. "I don't want you to be disappointed."

Mr. Moose had been listening to her and nodded earnestly. But when Mama turned away he grinned at me, showing all his huge white teeth.

Smothered in soot, Santerclaws turned to Mama saying, "Madam, we're in a terrible rush, but all the same I would like to have a wash before we set off."

"Let's all go inside," said Mama. "Grandma will run a bath and make hot chocolate."

"Wonderful," sighed Santerclaws. "Though a little drop of cherry brandy before we set off would go down very well, too."

Grandma didn't come out into the garden with us when we were saying good-bye to Mr. Moose and Santerclaws. I believe that she was actually a bit frightened of Mr. Moose because he was so huge.

Mama had turned the lights on in every room in

the house. Light shone out from every window and snowflakes sailed past them like golden feathers.

Gertrude Wutherspoon said her women's group could go jump in a lake, and gave Mr. Moose a big hug. Then she took off her most beautiful scarf and tied it around his neck.

"Don't you look smart, Moose!" said Santerclaws. "That'll really make you stand out when you pull the Christmas sled tomorrow."

Mr. Moose snorted. His nostrils began to quiver and I saw his legs were trembling. "Boss," he stammered. "What an honor! But what will the reindeer—"

"I'll take care of them," interrupted Santerclaws. It was meant to sound stern, but I could see he was trying not to laugh.

Oh, I was so proud of my beloved Mr. Moose, who didn't know where to look he was so embarrassed. His deepest wish had come true, and on top of it, he was given a jar of poached pears that Mama had packed for him.

"Those are to have on the way," Mama said to Mr. Moose.

"Madam," said Mr. Moose formally, "when I consume these I shall neither slurp nor burp."

"Burps aren't so bad," said Mama with a smile.

Kiki's present for Mr. Moose was one of the photos she'd taken for the insurance. Then she looked down. She can't bear to be seen crying.

"We'll always have Paris," said Mr. Moose. "Here's looking at you, kid."

That was nice of him, as those were the last words in the film *Casablanca* that Kiki had thought so romantic. Only it wasn't Kiki who was flying away, but Mr. Moose.

"I don't even have a jelly bear for you, Mr. Moose," I said sadly as he turned to me. "I haven't got anything at all."

"Yes, you have. But you already gave it to me."

One last time I put my arms around his warm neck and tickled him behind his enormous ears. "Good-bye, Mr. Moose," I whispered.

"Good-bye, little boy," said Mr. Moose. Then he went down on his knees to let Santerclaws climb up on his back.

I just can't describe what was going on inside me at that moment. I was being brave and didn't cry, because Mr. Moose had once said it broke his heart to see little boys cry. My own heart didn't break. It burst into a thousand little splinters, like Søren when Mr. Moose landed on it.

The air flickered as Santerclaws scattered the last of the remaining Milky Way Powder from the little bag over Mr. Moose.

"Keep well, keep well, and Happy Christmas," Santerclaws called.

Mr. Moose scraped his hooves on the ground and in the next moment he and Santerclaws had already disappeared in the dark winter sky as if they'd never been here.

Kiki put her arm round me. "Let's go inside and wrap up the juicer."

So that is the story of Mr. Moose. I've written it down to show everyone why I believe in Father Christmas and the flying elk. It's just as well I finished it in time, because I've promised Mama to decorate the Christmas tree.

My story certainly isn't scientific like Kiki's account of the life of the elks. I can hear her clacking away at the typewriter next door. With a bit of luck her work will get her accepted by the Académie française.

Today it's Christmas Eve and later on Papa is

coming to see us. Mama is downstairs in the kitchen baking cakes. Grandma's helping her, although she's still offended about the coconut biscuits. From time to time Mama bursts out laughing. I think she's very excited.

I'm excited, too. Perhaps Mama and Papa will get on well together again. Perhaps Papa will stay with us.

That's my Christmas wish.

I hope Mr. Moose hasn't forgotten about us.